JOAN IRVINE

Make Your Own Pop-ups

ANGUS
& ROBERTSON
PUBLISHERS

*This book is dedicated
both to my family — Steven,
Seth and Elly — and to the
hundreds of school children
whom I have taught who know
me as The Pop-up Lady.*

Acknowledgements
*I would like to acknowledge the
support of the Ontario Arts Council
through the program Creative Artists
in Schools. As a result of receiving
Ontario Arts Council grants and
teaching hundreds of students the
art of making pop-up books in
twelve schools throughout Grey and
Bruce Counties, I have had the
opportunity to explore and develop
pop-up construction with many
children.*

 *Thank you to the many children
in schools who tested and invented
new pop-up techniques.*

 *My own children helped me
enormously with sections of the
book. A thank you to my husband for
his support and patience during the
project.*

 *A great thank you goes to my
editor, Sarah Swartz, who helped me
in rewriting and improving the
original manuscript.*

 *Finally, I would like to
acknowledge the helpful advice and
encouragement of Val Wyatt, Valerie
Hussey and Ricky Englander of Kids
Can Press.*

Introduction

If you've ever seen a pop-up book or card, you'll know how special they are. Suddenly a figure comes alive by leaping out at you or moving across the page. Pop-ups are full of surprises, magic and fun.

This book will show you how to make your very own pop-ups. You may need a birthday card for a friend or some party invitations. You may want to make your own cards for Mother's Day, Valentine's Day, Halloween or other holidays. Your family and friends will love them, and you will have the satisfaction of knowing you made them yourself. Using the ideas in this book, you can even make a centrepiece or a free-standing object for a school project.

By making your own pop-ups, you will be carrying on a very long tradition. In the 1700s, "novelty books" with flaps, peepholes and cut-outs were produced to amuse children. In the 1840s, greeting cards with simple pop-ups became popular. Valentine cards were made with flaps that opened to show a message or scene.

Making pop-ups is easy. First, choose a design that works best for your message. This book will give you suggestions for different types of pop-ups. After a while, you will find you are inventing your own pop-up ideas.

Next, carefully follow the instructions for cutting and folding. Your first pop-up will probably be the hardest to make, but with practice you will become an expert. Remember to take your time and be patient. And most important of all, have fun!

Materials

To make your pop-ups, you will need the following materials.

- *Glue* With light paper, use a glue stick. With heavy paper, use white glue. Always apply glue sparingly and keep glue clear of all moving parts of your pop-up. When you glue two pieces of paper together, a strip of glue on each edge is usually enough.

- *Paper* For cards that will last, use heavy paper like construction paper or light bristol board. Lighter weight paper can be used for pop-ups that don't get much wear and tear.

- *Cutting blade* A Stanley knife or any other kind of craft knife is useful for making a cut in the middle of a page. Ask an adult to help when you need to use a cutting blade.

- *Ruler* Use a ruler for measurements given in the instructions. A metal ruler will help you make crisp folds and guide your cutting blade.

- *Scissors* A sharp pair of scissors with pointed ends are good for cutting paper. Remember to use all cutting equipment with care.

- *Pencil, markers, crayons, coloured pencils, paints* Use an erasable pencil for marking measurements and for designing your drawings. Then go over your pencil drawings with colour.

- *String, rubber bands, fabrics, buttons, ribbons, gift wrap, feathers, magazines* These materials and others can be glued to your pop-ups as decorations.

Symbols and Definitions

The following symbols and definitions will be useful to you when you use this book.

- Flap — a small piece of paper that hangs loose

- Tab — a small paper insert that can be glued or pulled

- Spring — a folded device that makes an object pop up

- Mountain fold — an upward fold, shaped like a mountain

- Valley fold — a downward fold, shaped like a valley

- Accordion fold — an up-down-up fold or a down-up-down fold, shaped like a fan

- Fold line – – – – – –

- Cut line ———

- Draw

- Colour

- Measure

- Glue

Tips for Folding and Scoring

To make a straight fold on heavy paper, score the paper first. Scoring means making a crease on your paper along the line to be folded. Lay a metal ruler near the line to be folded. Then carefully run the blunt end of a pair of scissors or a ball-point pen without ink along the fold line. Some people score their paper by running a fingernail across the fold line. When you fold your paper, remember to press firmly.

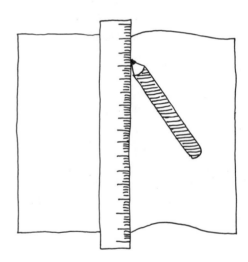

Tips for Cutting

You will need a sharp pair of scissors for most activities in this book. If you are making a cut in the middle of a page, use a pair of pointed scissors to puncture one of the corners of the cut line before cutting.

A cutting blade, such as a Stanley knife, works best to make a cut in the middle of a page. Be careful when using a cutting blade. Adult supervision is recommended.

When you use a cutting blade, a metal ruler will help you to guide the knife down the side of the ruler. Always put a board or a thick piece of cardboard under your work, so that you don't damage your work space.

Tips for Measuring

All measurements are given in both metric and imperial systems. When you follow the instructions for making a pop-up, start with one system and stay with it for the whole activity. Measurements differ slightly from system to system.

Part One
PUSH AND POP OUT

Would you like to make a talking creature or a valentine for your friend? You will find the ideas in Part One.

With push and pop-out cards, you will be cutting, folding and pushing a shape through to the other side of your paper. Your shape will pop out from the middle or the top of the page.

Some push and pop-out cards have the same kind of cuts and folds. The pop-up strip and the cage have straight, horizontal cuts. The triangle pop-up, the nose, the valentine and the opening flower have triangle shaped push-out areas.

Tips

● After you fold your paper in half, always cut on the *folded edge.*

● After you cut your paper, make *firm* folds by going over the fold lines with your thumb and index finger.

● It is easier to push your cut shape through to the other side, if you hold your paper like a tent.

● If you close your card and press firmly, the cut shape will remain pushed through to the other side of the paper.

● When you glue the inside and outside cards together, apply glue only to the outer edges of the inside card.

● Never apply glue near the pop-up shape.

Make a Pop-up Strip

1 Take two pieces of paper, each 21.5 cm × 28 cm (8½ in. × 11 in.). Fold each paper in half. Put one paper aside.

2 In the middle of the *folded edge* of the other paper, mark two dots, 1 cm (¼ in.) apart.

3 Starting at the dots, draw two parallel lines towards the edge of the paper. Each line should be 2.5 cm (1 in.) long.

4 Cut the lines starting from the folded edge.

5 Fold the cut strip back and then fold it forward again.

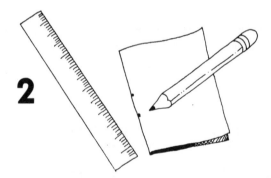

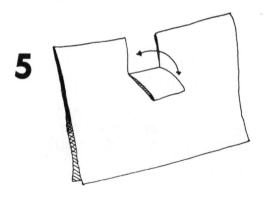

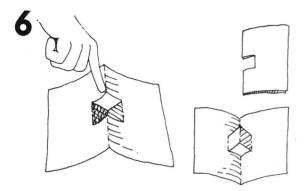

6 Open your card and hold it like a tent. Push the strip through to the other side of your card. Close the card and press firmly. Open to see the pop-up strip.

7 Draw a person or animal on a sheet of paper. The figure can be a little taller and wider than your strip. Colour in the figure. Then cut it out.

8 Apply glue on one side of the strip. Place the figure on the glue.

9 Now glue your card to the paper you put aside, which now becomes the outside of your card. When you open your card, the little cut-out figure will pop up.

10 Decorate the front and inside of your card.

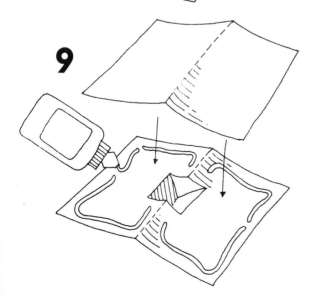

More Pop-up Strips

HOUSE SHAPE

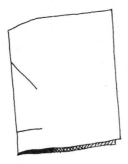 

EGG SHAPE

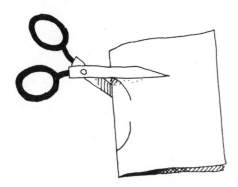 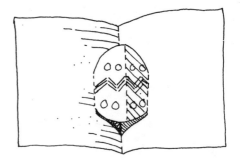

BUTTERFLY SHAPE

You can make more than one strip in the middle of your card. Each strip can be a different size.

You can also stick figures on both sides of your strip.

Have fun by adding more paper to your strips.

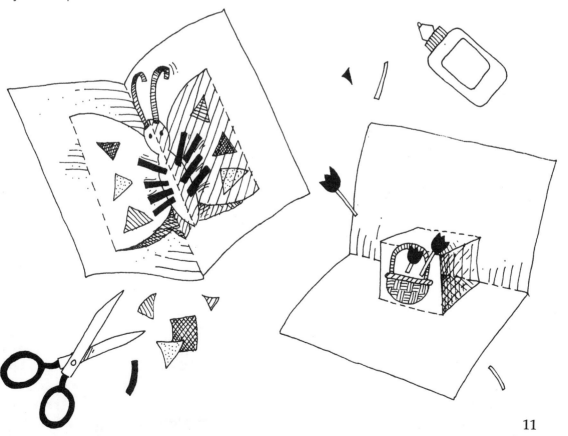

Triangle Pop-ups

1 Take two pieces of paper, each 21.5 cm × 28 cm (8½ in. × 11 in.). Fold each paper in half. Put one aside.

2 Place the other paper so that the folded edge is on your left. Fold the top corner to make a triangle.

3 Unfold the triangle and open the card. You will see an upside-down triangle at the top of your page. Pull the triangle towards you. Press the fold lines in the opposite direction of the original folds, so that the triangle points forward.

4 When you close the card, it will look like diagram 4.

1

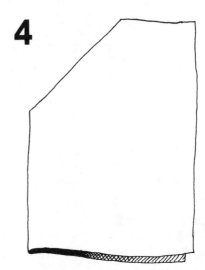

2

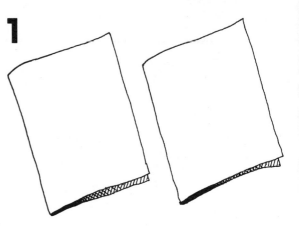

3

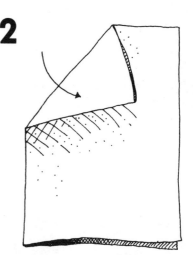

4

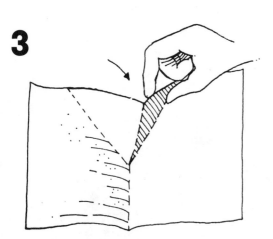

5

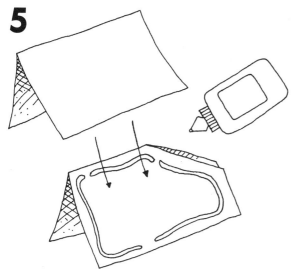

5 Apply glue to the outside of your card. Glue it to the paper you put aside, which now becomes the outside of your card. *Make sure you do not apply glue in the pop-up triangle area.*

6 Take a piece of paper that is 5 cm × 7 cm (2 in. × 2¾ in.). Draw a figure on this paper. It could be a person, an animal or an object. Colour it and cut it out.

7 Fold the figure in half vertically. Apply glue on the bottom area of the back of your figure. Place the figure on the triangle, so that the folds match and the top part of the figure is above your card.

8 Now decorate the front and inside of your card.

6

7

8

on
HALLOWE'EN
NIGHT...

YOU MIGHT
GET A
FRIGHT!

Make a Talking Mouth

1 Take two pieces of paper, each 21.5 cm × 28 cm (8½ in. × 11 in.). Fold each paper in half. Put one aside.

2 On the other, put a dot in approximately the centre of the folded edge.

3 Draw a 5 cm (2 in.) line from the dot towards the outer edge.

4 Starting at the folded edge, cut on the line.

5 Fold back the flaps to form two triangles.

6 Open up the flaps again. Open the whole page.

1

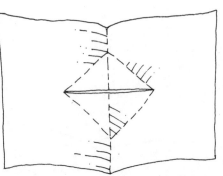

2

3

4

5

6

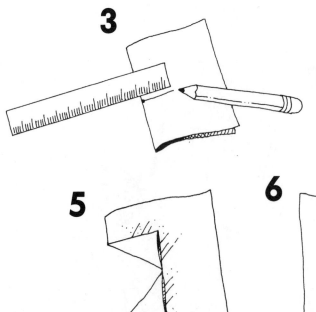

7

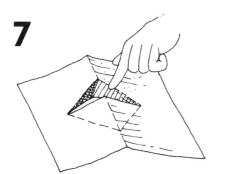

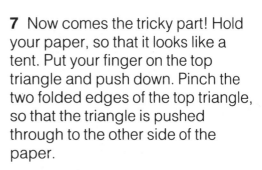

7 Now comes the tricky part! Hold your paper, so that it looks like a tent. Put your finger on the top triangle and push down. Pinch the two folded edges of the top triangle, so that the triangle is pushed through to the other side of the paper.

8 Put your finger on the bottom triangle and do the same thing. The top and bottom triangles will now be pushed out to form a mouth inside the card. When you open and close your card, the mouth will look like it is talking. When your card is closed, it will look like diagram 8.

8

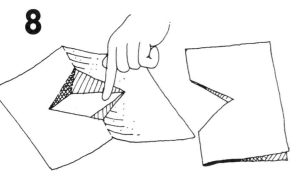

9 Draw a monster, a person or an animal around your mouth.

10 Glue the inside and outside cards together. *Do not apply glue in the area of the pop-up mouth.* You now have a cover for your card.

9

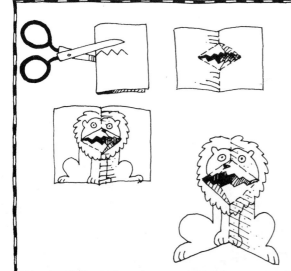

10

Other Ideas
Your card can also be a centrepiece for a table, if you use heavy paper.

1 Draw a jagged line, instead of a straight line, for the talking mouth. Your figure will now have teeth.

2 Draw a head and body around the mouth. Make sure the body is wider than the head, so that your figure can stand.

3 Cut around the figure's head and body to make a centrepiece.

Make a Pop-up Valentine

1 Take two pieces of paper, each 21.5 cm × 28 cm (8½ in. × 11 in.). Fold each paper in half. Put one aside.

2 Place the other paper so that the folded edge is on your left. Fold the top corner to make a large triangle.

3 Fold back the triangle. Draw the top part of half a heart from the folded edge to the triangle fold.

4 Cut the top part of the valentine, stopping at the triangle fold mark.

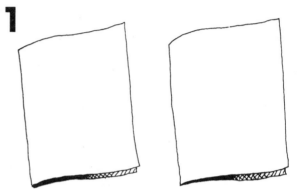

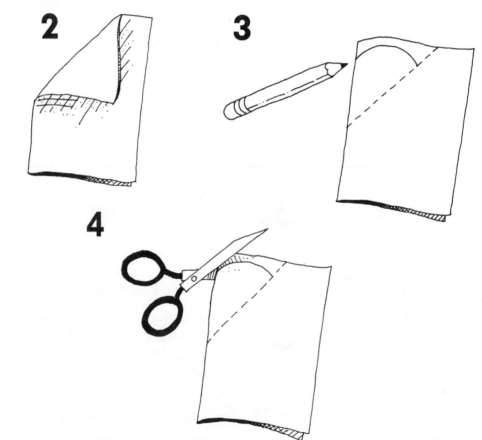

5 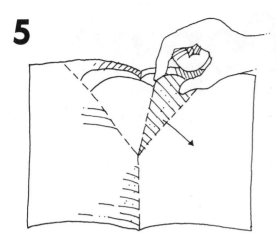 Open the card and pull the valentine towards you. Press the fold lines so that the valentine points forward.

6 Colour the valentine.

7 Apply glue to the outside of your card. Glue it to the paper you put aside. *Do not apply glue in the area of the pop-up heart.*

8 Decorate the front of your card.

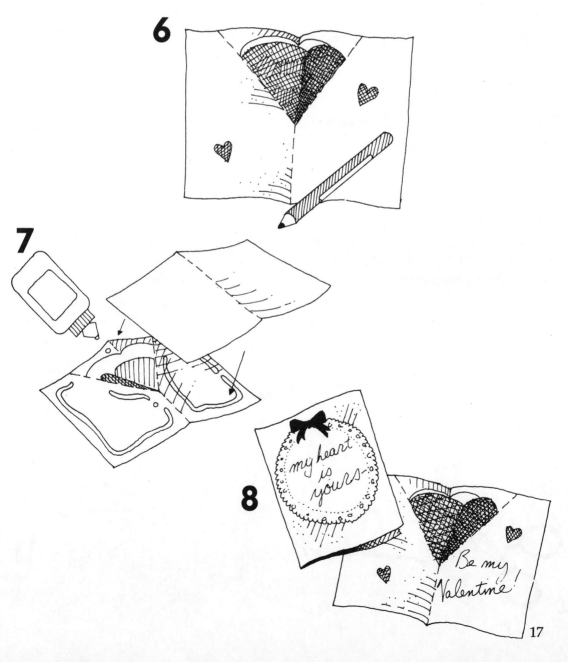

Make a Pop-up Nose

1 Take two pieces of paper, each 21.5 cm × 28 cm (8½ in. × 11 in.). Fold each paper in half. Put one aside.

2 Place the other paper so that the folded edge is on your left. Fold the bottom corner to make a large triangle.

3 Fold back the triangle. Draw a curved line from the folded edge to the triangle fold. Then cut along this curved line, stopping at the triangle fold mark.

4 Open the card. You will see a nose shape. Pull the nose towards you. Press the fold lines, so that the nose points towards you.

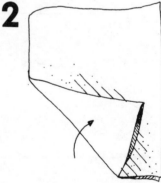

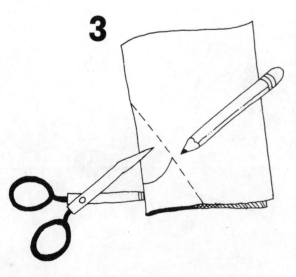

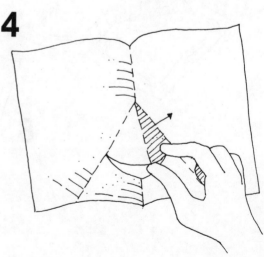

5 Glue the inside and outside cards together. *Do not apply glue in the area of the pop-up nose.*

6 Draw a face around the nose. Decorate the front of your card.

5

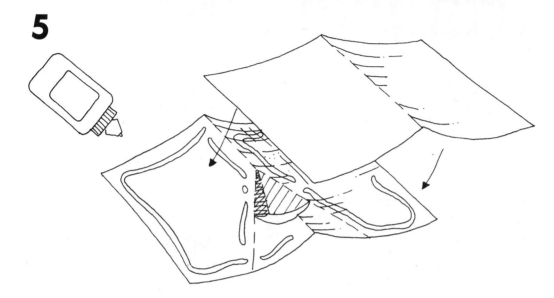

6

More Triangle Folds

VASE OF FLOWERS

1 Make a pop-up valentine shape. (See page 16.)

2 Draw, colour and cut out several flowers.

3 Attach paper flowers to the inside of the valentine. Colour the valentine vase.

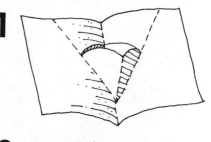

ANGEL

1 Make a pop-up nose shape. (See page 18.)

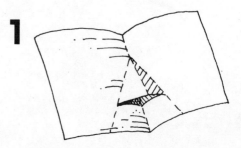

2

2 Draw a head with a halo at the top of this triangle shape. Add wings and hands. Colour the triangle. It becomes the angel's dress.

3 Draw, colour and cut out two feet. Attach feet to the bottom of the triangle.

3

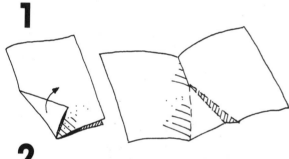

1

UMBRELLA

1 Make a triangle fold at the bottom of a piece of paper.

2 Colour the triangle so that it looks like an umbrella.

3 Draw, colour and cut out a handle. Glue the handle to the inside of the bottom triangle at one side of the fold line.

2

3

Make an Open Flower

1 Take two pieces of paper, each 21.5 cm × 28 cm (8½ in. × 11 in.). Fold each paper in half. Put one aside.

2 Fold the other paper again, so that it is folded in quarters.

3 Open the paper, so that it is folded in half. Take the top left corner and fold to the centre line. Take the bottom left corner and fold to the centre line.

4 Open the paper, so that it is folded in half again.

5 With a pencil, draw a curved line from the folded side to the top fold line. Draw a second curved line from the folded side to the bottom fold line. Cut along both curved lines.

1

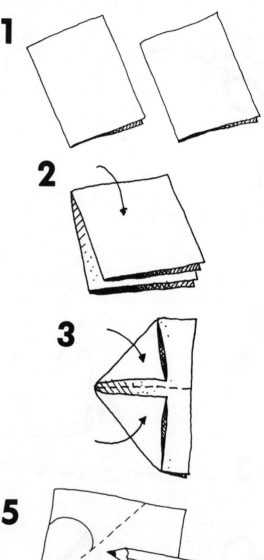

2

3

4

5

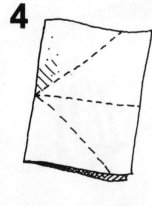

6

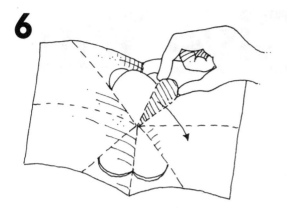

6 Open the paper. You will see two triangles with shapes inside. Pull the shape inside the top triangle towards you. Press the fold lines, so that the shape stands out. Do the same with the shape inside the bottom triangle.

7 When your card is closed, these two shapes, which are the petals of your flower, are tucked inside your card.

8 Now draw the other petals on your flower. Colour your flower.

9 Glue the inside and outside cards together. *Do not apply glue in the area of the pop-up petals.*

10 Decorate the front and inside of your card.

7

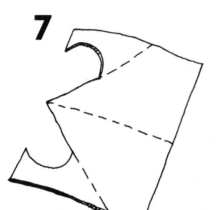

9

8

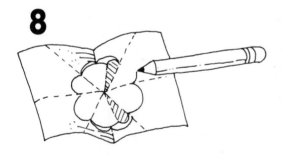

10

roses are red,
violets are blue...

here is
a flower

just for
you!

Let me Give You a Hug!

1 Take two pieces of paper, each 21.5 cm × 28 cm (8½ in. × 11 in.). Fold each paper in half. Put one aside. Fold the other paper again, so that it is folded in quarters.

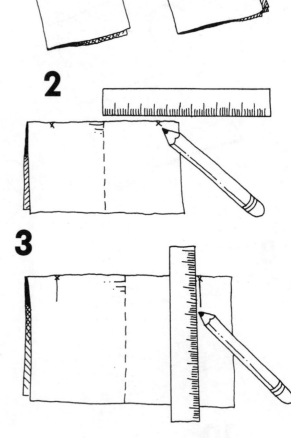

2 Open the paper, so that it is folded in half. Place the folded edge at the top. Starting where the fold lines meet, measure 8 cm (3⅛ in.) on either side of the middle fold line. Mark these points with an ×.

3 From each ×, draw a vertical line that is 1.6 cm (⅝ in.) long.

4 At the bottom of each vertical line, draw a horizontal line towards the middle fold, that is 6 cm (2½ in.) long. Cut all the lines.

5 Measure 0.5 cm (⅛ in.) on either side of the middle fold and mark these points with a dot. Draw a dotted line from each dot to the end of each cut line.

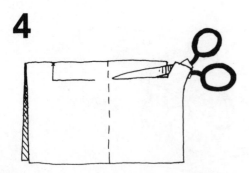

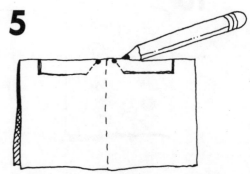

6

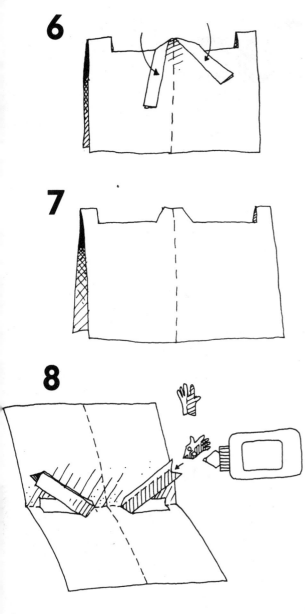

6 Fold the cut pieces towards the centre, along the dotted lines. Press the folds firmly. Fold the cut pieces back again.

7 Open your paper and hold it like a tent. Push the cut pieces through to the other side of the paper. Press the fold lines in the opposite direction of the original folds, so that your shape is now folded with the peaks towards you. When you open your card, two arms will pop out. When you close your card, it will look like diagram 7.

8 Cut out two mittens or hands, each about 3 cm (1¼ in.) long. Fold them down the middle lengthways. Glue them to the arms so that the fold lines match.

9 Apply glue to the back of your card. Place the card on the paper you have put aside. *Make sure you do not apply glue in the area of the arms.*

10 Draw and colour a body, head and legs for your woman or man. By opening and closing your card, the person will give you a hug.

THANK-YOU!

Make a Cage or a Jail

1 Take two pieces of paper, each 21.5 cm × 28 cm (8½ in. × 11 in.). Fold each paper in half. Put one aside.

2 Along the folded edge of the other paper, draw 12 dots that are 1 cm (⅜ in.) apart. The dots should be in the middle section of the folded edge, beginning 5 cm (2 in.) from the edge of the page.

3 Using a ruler, draw a straight line, 7 cm (2¾ in.) long, from the first dot towards the edge of the paper. Draw another line, 7 cm (2¾ in.) long, from the last dot.

4 From all the other dots, draw lines, 6 cm (2¼ in.) long. Keep them as parallel to each other as possible.

5 Join the long lines with a dotted line. Join the shorter lines with a solid line.

6 Starting at the folded edge, cut all the vertical lines. Shade in each second space that has a solid line across the bottom.

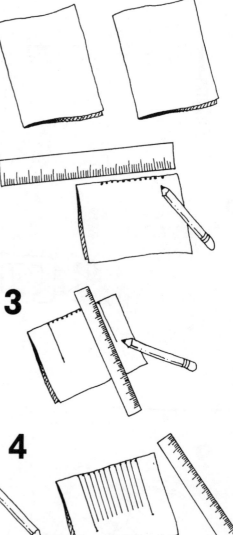

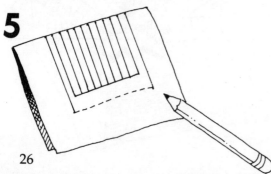

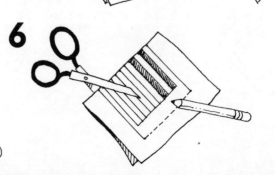

7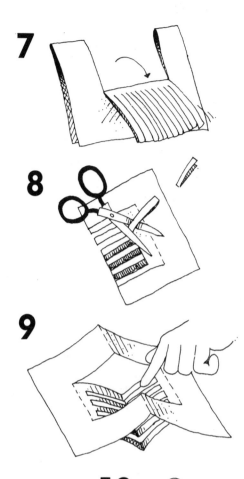

7 Fold the entire inside section along the dotted line. Fold this area back again.

8 Now cut out all the shaded areas.

9 Open your paper and hold it like a tent. Push the cut section down in the opposite direction of the fold, so that the bars are pushed through to the other side. Close your card with the cut section inside and press firmly. Open your card. The bars on the cage will stand out.

10 Glue the inside and outside papers together. *Do not apply glue in the area of the bars.*

11 Now draw, colour and cut out an animal or person to put in your cage or jail. Make sure to include a tab at the bottom of your figure. Your figure should be glued by its tab inside the cage, facing the bars.

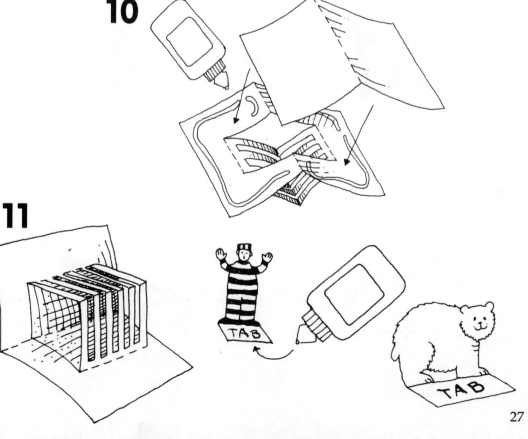

Part Two

FOLD
AND
FIT IN

Imagine making a mountain scene with a tiny mountain climber or a little bedroom card with a "Get Well" message. There are many cards that are fun to make in Part Two.

With fold and fit-in cards, you will be cutting and folding a figure or scene. You will then be fitting and gluing it into the middle of the card. The glued figures will pop out when you open your card.

Part Two uses different kinds of folds, such as a mountain fold, a valley fold and an accordion fold. It also uses springs, sometimes called Jacob's Ladder, to make figures pop up.

Some of the cards in this section have similar ways of working. With some ideas, you will be folding a piece of paper a number of times, cutting it and then gluing it into the middle of your card. Sometimes, you will be gluing a structure, such as a mountain, into the middle of the card on the fold line to create an interesting scene.

Tips

● With figures that are cut and folded, such as the cut-out dolls, apply glue on the bottom of the folded piece and place it near the middle fold of your page. Then apply glue on the top and close your card.

● Make sure you allow the glue to dry, before you open the card carefully to see your figure pop out.

● Don't be discouraged if your card does not close properly. Gently loosen the glued areas and try placing the folded piece in again more carefully.

● Usually figures will pop up if they are folded in half and have a base that is V-shaped. Make sure that the middle of the V-shaped base is placed directly on the fold line of your paper.

29

Make a Pop-up Cube or Box

1 Fold a piece of paper, 21.5 cm × 14 cm (8½ in. × 5½ in.), in half. Put it aside. This will be your card.

2 Cut a strip of paper, 4 cm × 16 cm (1½ in. × 6¼ in.). Fold the strip in half lengthways. Then fold the strip in half again. Open the strip and you will have three folds.

3 Cut a 1 cm (¼ in.) piece off both ends of your strip.

4 Fold the strip on the lines with mountain folds. A *mountain fold* is upward like a mountain △. You will now have a cube shape.

5 Open the cube with the peaks of the folds up. Put glue on both end sections of the strip.

6 Fold the strip into a cube again. Place the cube into the centre of your paper, an equal distance from the top and bottom. Line up the middle fold in the strip with the fold in your paper. The ends of the strip *should not* meet in the middle fold. Make sure that your card opens and closes easily.

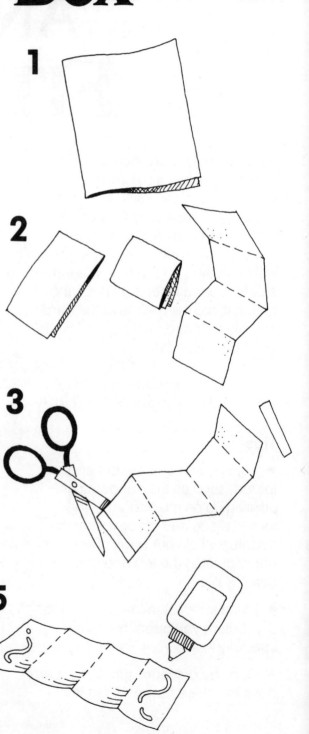

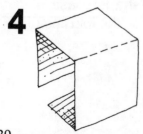

6

7

7 Draw a figure that is a little taller than one side of your cube. Colour and cut out the figure.

8 Glue it to one side of your cube, making sure that the bottom of your figure is no lower than the bottom of your cube. When your card closes, the figure should be completely inside your card.

9 Decorate the front and inside of your card.

9

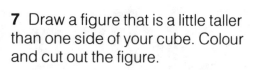

8

Other Ideas

By using the paper as a vertical card, you can cut out a little figure and glue it *inside* the cube. When you make the figure, cut it out and then fold it in half. Put glue on the front bottom half of the figure. Match the fold lines of the figure with the fold lines of the cube.

Folding Figures

1 Fold a heavy piece of paper, 21.5 cm × 14 cm (8½ in. × 5½ in.), in half. Put it aside. This will be your card.

2 Cut a strip of paper, 17 cm × 7 cm (7 in. × 2¾ in.). Make the following measurements on the strip, from left to right: 3 cm, 6 cm, 2 cm, and 6 cm (1¼ in., 2½ in., ¾ in., 2½ in.). From each mark, draw a vertical line on your strip. Make sure that sections 2 and 4 are the same size.

3 Choose a scene such as a bed, a car or a sofa that can be divided into three sections. Draw and colour your scene on the first three sections of your folded paper. The fourth section is a blank tab. A *tab* is a section of paper that will be attached to another piece of paper. You do not draw on the tabs. Make the folds indicated on the diagram. Remember, a *mountain fold* is upward like a mountain⬒. A *valley fold* is downward like a valley ⬓.

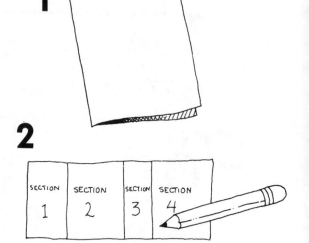

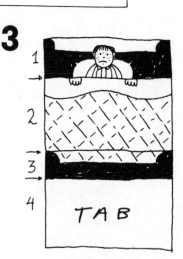

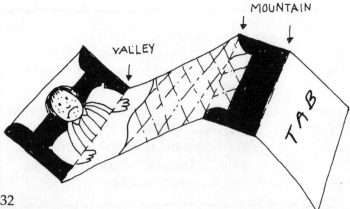

4 Apply glue on the front side of the tab. Fold the tab back and place it on the bottom section of your folded paper, with the edge of the tab on the fold line of the paper.

5 Apply glue behind the top section and close your card. Press down firmly. Wait for the glue to dry. Open the card carefully. The top section should now be glued in place. The figure or scene will collapse when the card is closed. It will pop open when the card is opened.

6 Decorate the front and inside of your card.

Other Ideas
You can make an animal or a figure pop out in the same way. Add a tab to the bottom of the figure. Fold the figure together with the tab into four sections. Glue it to your page.

Make a Snake

1 Fold a heavy piece of paper, 21.5 cm × 14 cm (8½ in. × 5½ in.), in half. Put it aside. This will be your card.

2 Take a heavy piece of paper, 10 cm × 10 cm (4 in. × 4 in.), and draw a spiral on it.

3 Turn the spiral into a snake, by adding eyes to the inside section. Colour your snake. You can add an interesting pattern to your colouring.

4 Cut out the spiral. Carefully decorate the back of the spiral.

5 Apply glue behind the snake's head (centre of the spiral).

1

2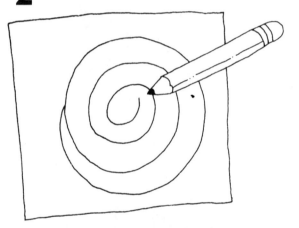

3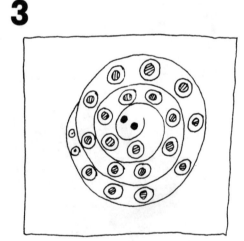

4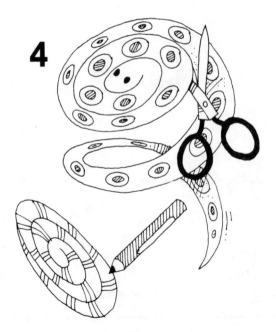

5

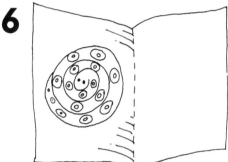

6 Place the whole snake in the middle of the left side of the folded page, glue side down. Allow the glue to dry.

7 Apply a small amount of glue on the snake's tail (end of spiral). Close your card carefully and press it firmly. Allow the glue to dry. Open the card carefully. The tail should be glued in place.

8 Add a tongue to your snake.

9 Decorate the front and inside of your card.

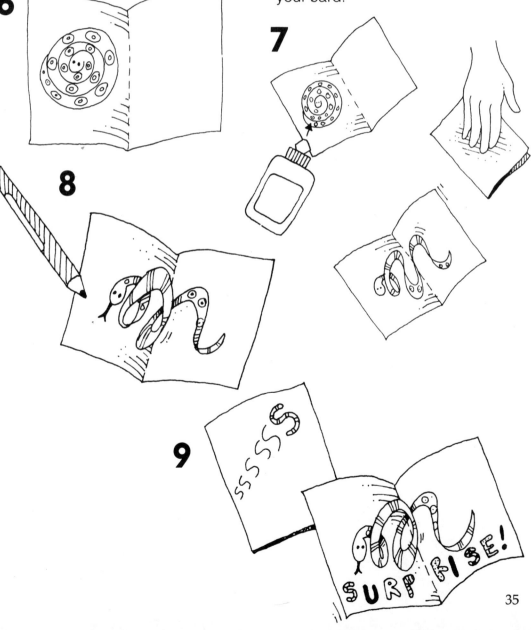

Cut-out Shapes

1 Fold a heavy piece of paper, 21.5 cm × 14 cm (8½ in. × 5½ in.), in half. Put it aside. This will be your card.

2 Cut a strip of paper, 21.5 cm × 7 cm (8½ in. × 2¾ in.). Fold it in half. Then accordion fold it. An *accordion fold* is an up-down-up fold or a down-up-down fold. Your strip should have three folds.

3 Close the strip and draw a figure on the top section. It can be a person, animal or object. Make sure that the hands or feet of your figure run off both sides of the section, so that your figures in each section will be connected.

4 Cut and open the strip. The middle two figures should bend towards you. Colour the figures.

1

2

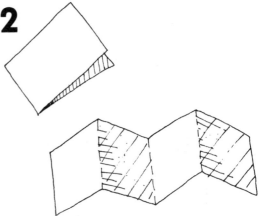

3

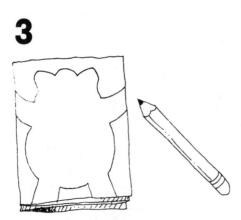

4

5 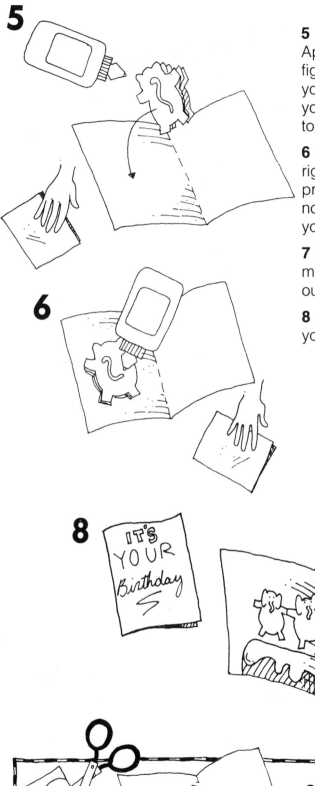 Fold the figures together again. Apply glue on the back of the far left figure and place it on the left side of your card, near the middle fold of your page. Press firmly and allow it to dry.

6 Apply glue on the back of the far right figure. Close your card and press firmly. The far right figure will now be glued to the right side of your card. Allow the glue to dry.

7 When you open your card, the middle two figures will be standing out.

8 Decorate the front and inside of your card.

7

8

IT'S
YOUR
Birthday

HOW COULD I
FORGET?!

IT'S ME ❤ YOU!

Other Ideas
For an interesting Valentine card, make cut-out hearts and glue them inside a card. Make sure the sides of your hearts are connected.

Make a Mountain or a Tent

1 Fold a heavy piece of paper, 21.5 cm × 14 cm (8½ in. × 5½ in.), in half. You will be making a mountain or tent with this paper.

2 Place the paper down, so that the fold is on your left. Mark a dot on the bottom edge of the page, 10 cm (4 in.) from the folded corner. Mark a dot on the folded edge, 10 cm (4 in.) up from the folded bottom corner. Using a ruler, draw a line between the dots.

3 Cut along this line. Open the paper and you will have a triangle.

4 Place the triangle down so that the longest side is on the bottom. Fold the bottom edge up 1.2 cm (½ in.), so that your triangle looks like a hat.

5 Fold the bottom edge down. Mark with a dot the spot where the fold lines meet. Starting at the dot, draw a little triangle at the bottom of your large triangle. Cut out the little triangle. You now have two tabs at the bottom of the mountain.

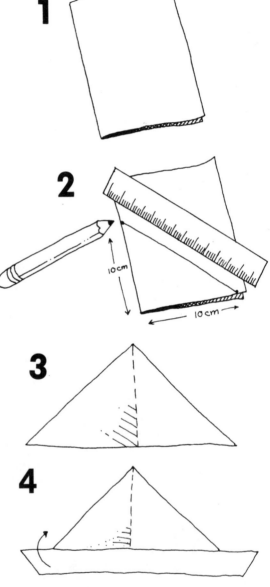

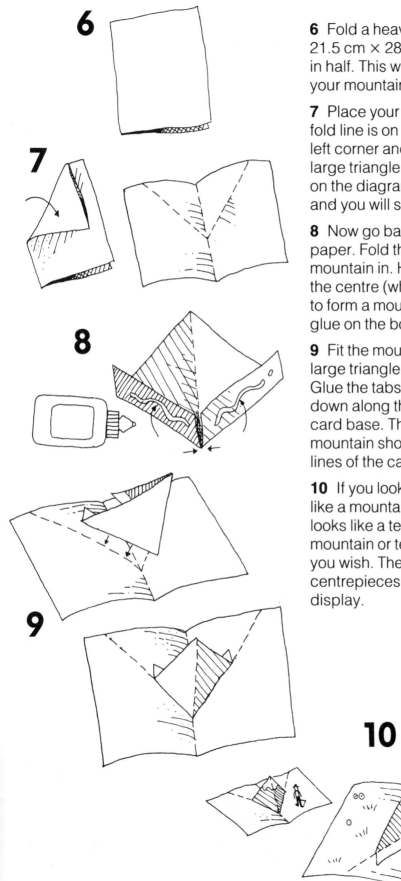

6 Fold a heavy piece of paper, 21.5 cm × 28 cm (8½ in. × 11 in.), in half. This will be the card base for your mountain or tent.

7 Place your card base so that the fold line is on the left. Take the top left corner and fold it over to make a large triangle. See the proportions on the diagram. Open your paper and you will see a large triangle.

8 Now go back to your mountain paper. Fold the bottom tabs of your mountain in. Have the tabs meet in the centre (where you drew the dot) to form a mountain shape. Apply glue on the bottom of both tabs.

9 Fit the mountain shape into the large triangle on your card base. Glue the tabs of your mountain down along the triangle lines of your card base. The fold lines of the mountain should line up with the fold lines of the card base.

10 If you look at it one way, it looks like a mountain. Turn it around and it looks like a tent. Now decorate your mountain or tent. Add little figures if you wish. These scenes make good centrepieces for a table or a display.

Make a Trapeze

1 Fold a heavy piece of paper, 21.5 cm × 14 cm (8½ in. × 5½ in.), in half. Put it aside. This will be your card.

2 Cut two strips of heavy paper, each 12 cm × 7 cm (4¾ in. × 2¾ in.).

3 Fold both strips of paper in half lengthwise.

4 On the fold line of each strip, draw a line 4 cm (1½ in.) long. Open the paper and cut the line on both strips.

5 Refold one strip. Fold both sections back as far as you have cut. Turn the piece over and fold the other cut section back. If you turn your piece of paper around, you will have a T-shape.

6

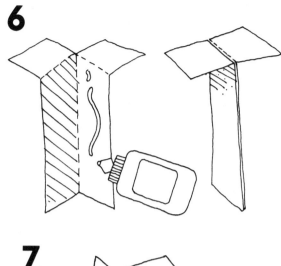

6 Apply glue in the middle of the long section of the T-shape and close the paper. Press firmly. Make another T-shape by repeating steps 5 and 6 with your second strip.

7 Open the folded heavy piece of paper you put aside. Place one T-shape near the bottom end of the paper, so that the centre of the T is lined up with the fold line of the paper. Place the other T-shape near the other end of the paper along the fold line. Glue both T-shapes to the paper.

7

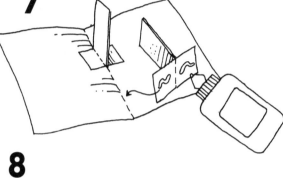

8 Now tape or glue the ends of a piece of string, a rubber band or a pipe-cleaner to the top of the T-shapes.

9 You can make a little man or woman swing on the string. Or you can make a little man or woman standing nearby, ready to jump.

8

9

sorry I couldn't make it...

Let's hang around together!

I had a swinging time !!

Other Ideas
You can make a person sitting on a swing. After you attach a pipe-cleaner or a long strip of paper to the tops of the T-shapes, add a swing and glue a little person to the swing.

Layered Bells or Angel's Dress

1 Fold a heavy piece of paper, 21.5 cm × 14 cm (8½ in. × 5½ in.), in half. Put it aside. This will be your card.

2 To make a bell pattern, take a piece of paper that is 10 cm × 14 cm (4 in. × 5½ in.). Fold it in half. Starting at the folded edge, draw half a bell. Cut out the shape and open it.

3 Take two pieces of paper, each 21.5 cm × 28 cm (8½ in. × 11 in.), each a different colour. Fold each paper in half. Then fold it in half again, so that your paper is divided into equal quarters. Lay your bell pattern on one folded paper and draw around it. Do the same with the other folded paper.

4 Cut the bell shape out of each folded paper. You should have eight bells altogether. Fold each bell shape in half.

5 Open the bell shapes and put them in a pile, alternating their colours, for example: red, green, red, green and so on. Staple or sew the bell shapes along the fold line. If you staple the bells, make sure that the staples are directly on the fold line.

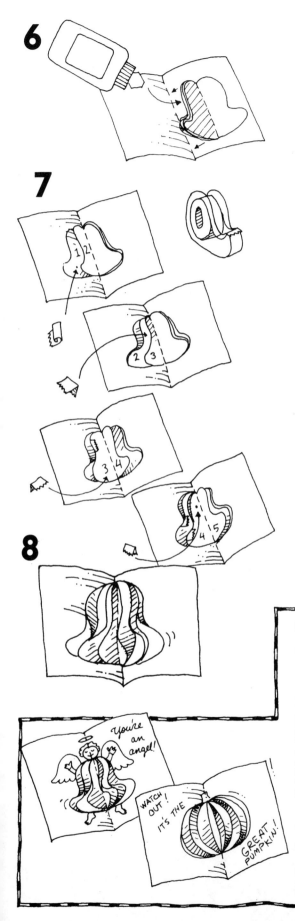

6 Apply glue on the bottom bell shape and place the pile of bell shapes in the middle of the heavy, folded piece of paper you have put aside. The fold lines should match. Allow the glue to dry.

7 Rip off 15 small pieces of sticky tape. Now you are ready for your taping!
Here is the pattern for taping. Start with the left bell, Bell 1, which has been glued down to the card.
  Tape:
  1. Bell 1 and Bell 2 at bottom. For the first two bells, roll the tape so that it is sticky on both sides.
  2. Bell 2 and Bell 3 in middle.
  3. Bell 3 and Bell 4 at bottom.
  4. Bell 4 and Bell 5 in middle.
  5. Bell 5 and Bell 6 at bottom.
  6. Bell 6 and Bell 7 in middle.
  7. Bell 7 and Bell 8 at bottom.
  For the last bell, roll the tape so that it is sticky on both sides.
When you open the card, you should have a layered bell.

8 Decorate your card.

Other Ideas
HALLOWEEN PUMPKIN

Instead of making a bell-shaped pattern, make a pumpkin-shaped pattern. Follow the instructions for the layered bell, using orange and yellow paper. When you are taping, you may want to use a lower piece of tape in the middle section.

ANGEL

You can use the bell shape as a dress for an angel. Draw an angel's head and wings.

Springs or Jacob's Ladder

1 Fold a heavy piece of paper, 21.5 cm × 14 cm (8½ in. × 5½ in.), in half. Put it aside. This will be your card.

2 Draw, colour and cut out a little figure on a piece of paper, 5 cm × 5 cm (2 in. × 2 in.). It could be an animal or person. This will be your object. Put it aside.

3 Cut out two strips of paper, each 7 cm × 1 cm (2¾ in. × ¼ in.).

4 Apply glue at the end of one strip of paper. Lay the other strip at right angles to the first strip on the glued area. Allow the glue to dry.

5 Bring the strip on the right side over to the left side and fold the edge. Bring the strip on the bottom up and over the glued area. Bring the strip on the left side over to the right side. Bring the strip on the top down to the bottom area. Continue overlapping the strips until all of the paper is folded.

1

2

3

4

5

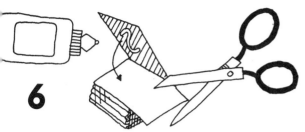

6 Apply glue under the top flap of paper and press the flap down. Cut off any extra paper.

7 Pull the spring out slightly. Apply glue on one end of the spring and attach it to the back of the figure.

8 Apply glue on the other end of the spring and attach the figure with the spring to your card.

9 Decorate the rest of your card.

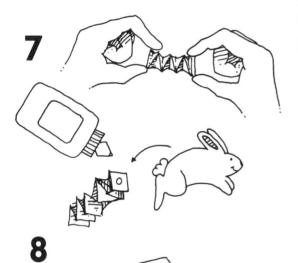

GUESS WHO'S BACK?

HAPPY HANUKKAH!

Other Ideas
If you make a large figure, you may want to make more than one spring to put under your figure.

More Springs

MAN WITH A CONCERTINA

1 Fold a heavy piece of paper, 21.5 cm × 14 cm (8½ in. × 5½ in.), in half. Put it aside. This will be your card.

2 Make a large spring using two strips of paper, each 2 cm × 28 cm (¾ in. × 11 in.).

3 Glue one end of the spring 0.3 cm (⅛ in.) away from the middle fold line of your card.

4 Apply glue on the top part of the spring and close your card. Press the card firmly for about a minute.

5 Open the card and you will see a spring that is pulled open. This will be the concertina.

6 Draw a man around the concertina. Add some musical notes to the page. Open and close your card and the man will play his concertina.

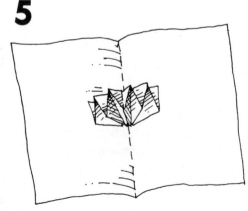

CROWN

1 Follow the instructions for the concertina. Instead of drawing a man, draw a face under the spring.

2 Decorate the crown by attaching stickers or sequins to the sides and top area of the spring.

HOLIDAY DECORATION

1 Take two strips of paper, 54 cm × 4 cm (21¼ in. × 1½ in.), each a different colour. If necessary, you can glue strips of paper together to make the long strips. Make a spring with the strips.

2 Apply glue on each end of the spring and attach both ends together. Add to your decoration with stickers and ribbons. Hang it on the wall, a Christmas tree or on a door.

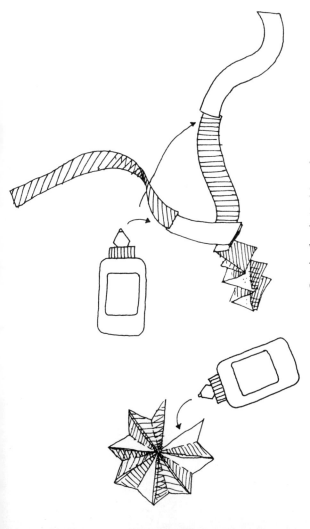

ANGUS & ROBERTSON PUBLISHERS

Unit 4, Eden Park, 31 Waterloo Road,
North Ryde, NSW, Australia 2113, and
16 Golden Square, London W1R 4BN,
United Kingdom

First published in Canada by
Kid's Can Press Ltd in 1987
as How to Make Pop-ups
First published in Australia
by Angus & Robertson Publishers in 1988
First published in the United Kingdom
by Angus & Robertson (UK) in 1988

Text copyright © 1987 by Joan Irvine
Illustrations copyright © 1987 by Barbara Reid

National Library of Australia
Cataloguing-in-publication data.

Irvine, Joan, 1951– .
  Make your own pop-ups.

  ISBN 0 207 15824 X.

  1. Paper work — Juvenile literature.
  2. Paper toy making — Juvenile literature.
  3. Creative activities and seatwork —
  Juvenile literature. I. Reid, Barbara,
  1957– . II. Title.

745.54

Typeset by Setrite Typesetters Ltd
Printed in Singapore